Clarissa
A True Fairy Tale

Story & Illustrations
by
Jennifer Flynn

Starlight Press
Beulah, Michigan

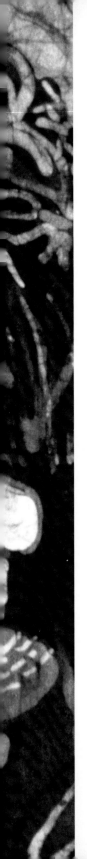

Rachel looked out the window and was sure that she could see Grandma sitting in her garden chair. Rachel went running through the house to find her mother. Her mother was in her studio drawing a picture of fairies dancing in a garden. Rachel looked closely at the picture and then said, "May I please go to Grandma's house?"

Her mother nodded and said, "Just be home for supper."

Rachel ran across the field to Grandma's house and found her in the garden. They hugged each other, and then Rachel said, "Grandma, will you please tell me the story about how you first met Clarissa?"

Grandma laughed and said, "Again?"

Rachel said, "Yes! Please can we go sit in the park in the same spot where Clarissa was sitting?"

Grandma said, "Okay, let's go!"

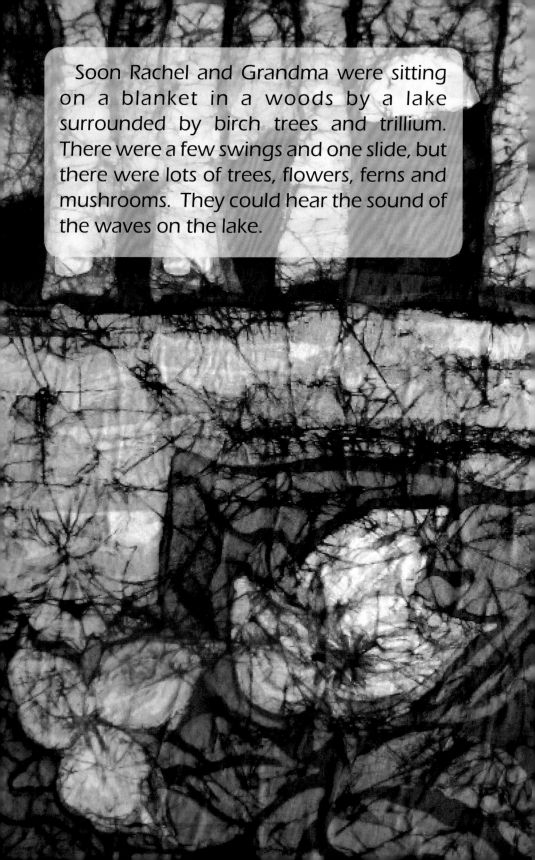

Soon Rachel and Grandma were sitting on a blanket in a woods by a lake surrounded by birch trees and trillium. There were a few swings and one slide, but there were lots of trees, flowers, ferns and mushrooms. They could hear the sound of the waves on the lake.

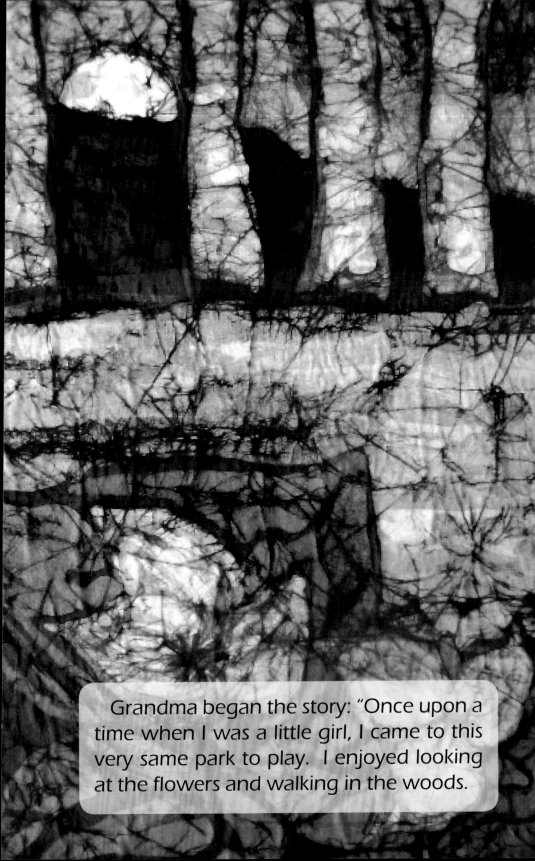

Grandma began the story: "Once upon a time when I was a little girl, I came to this very same park to play. I enjoyed looking at the flowers and walking in the woods.

One spring I was looking for trillium, lady slippers and marsh marigolds. I was bending down to look closer at a flower when the flower moved! It was not just a flower. It was a fairy holding a flower!

The fairy was tiny, with silver wings and golden hair and sat on a small rock. Then the fairy motioned for me to come closer. Just as I bent down, the fairy's hand flew up in the air, and pink, purple and blue fairy dust swirled around me. A rainbow of colors spun me all around until I was so dizzy I felt like I was falling.

Then I was standing next to the fairy, who had climbed down from the rock and was reaching out to shake my hand. "Hello," she said, "I'm pleased to meet you. I am Clarissa, and you are...?"

In a very shaky voice, I said "My name is Betty. What just happened?"

Clarissa said, "I just sprinkled you with fairy dust so that you could be my size. I have a very important place to go and I need you to come with me. Come on, don't just stand there. LET'S GO !!"

She grabbed my hand and we dashed straight into the woods. We reached a huge oak tree that had a teeny tiny door nestled between its roots.

Clarissa waved her wand, and the door opened. I walked into a beautiful room with a couch and chairs with flowers everywhere. There was the prettiest little kitchen with a tiny stove, miniature dishes and pots and pans.

Clarissa took down a teapot and made some blueberry tea. She reached into a jar and took out tiny frosted cookies with colorful icing. She placed everything on a little table and told me to sit down and eat. Those were the most delicious cookies I had ever eaten!

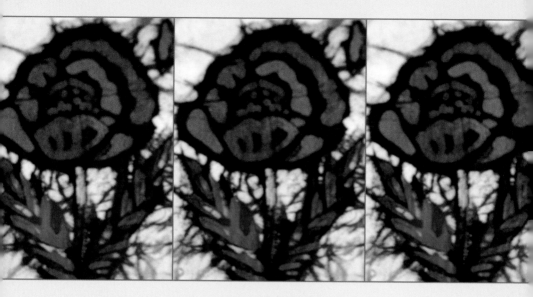

Then, Clarissa told me about the important place she had to go. She said that it was the first day of spring when all the fairies have a huge ball all night long. Every year there is a contest to see which fairy can bring the most unusual guest. Clarissa had been thinking about it all year and decided that she would bring a human girl. But she had to hide in the flowers patiently to find one on this important day. That human girl was me, and that was how I met Clarissa.

Then Clarissa jumped up, grabbed my hand and pulled me through another door.

"These are our dresses," she said.

"Oh my!" I said. I blinked my eyes three times and pinched my arm to find out if I were dreaming. I was standing in an amazing room. It was filled with the most beautiful dresses I had ever seen. They were the colors of the rainbow, sun, moon and stars. The dresses were gauzy and shiny with sparkling glitter. Under each dress, on the floor, were a matching pair of fairy slippers. There were boxes filled with jewelry and beautiful scarves that might have been spun from spider webs.

"Where did you get all these beautiful dresses?" I asked.

Clarissa said, "They are a gift from Mother Nature. Every time I do anything to help keep the world safe, she gives me a gift. For instance, one day I talked to some boys and girls at the beach and asked them to clean up the trash in the sand. They did, and the next day three new dresses were hanging outside my house with a note that said, "Good job," from Mother Nature. Now I spend all my time helping to keep our earth clean!"

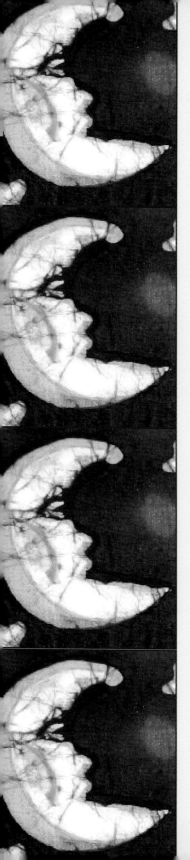

Then Clarissa waved her fairy wand in the air, and suddenly I was wearing a beautiful dress with matching shoes and a wreath of flowers on my head.

"Come on, let's go!" She grabbed my hand and we ran through the forest. It was dark out, but the moon and the stars glowed and lit our way.

When we got to the fairy circle, lots of other fairies were already dancing together. When they were not dancing, they were eating or playing hide and seek. I had the most wonderful time playing games with the fairies.

Clarissa won a flower petal necklace as the prize for having the most unusual guest. The fairies talked to me about saving the wildflowers and asked me to tell my friends not to pick Trillium or Lady Slippers. They said that those flowers are very fragile and need to be protected, because they are some of Mother Nature's precious gifts.

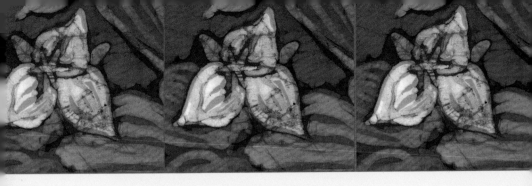

After the ball Clarissa and I went back to her tiny house in the tree, where I put my own clothes back on and sat on one of her chairs. I was so tired that I just fell asleep.

When I woke up, I was back at home in my own bed. I was still wearing the flower crown so I took it off and hung it on my wall. That flower wreath still hangs in my bedroom at home – and that is the end of that story.

"But Grandma, did you ever see Clarissa again?" Rachel asked.

"Oh yes, Rachel, many times, and we had many adventures together, but those are stories for another day."

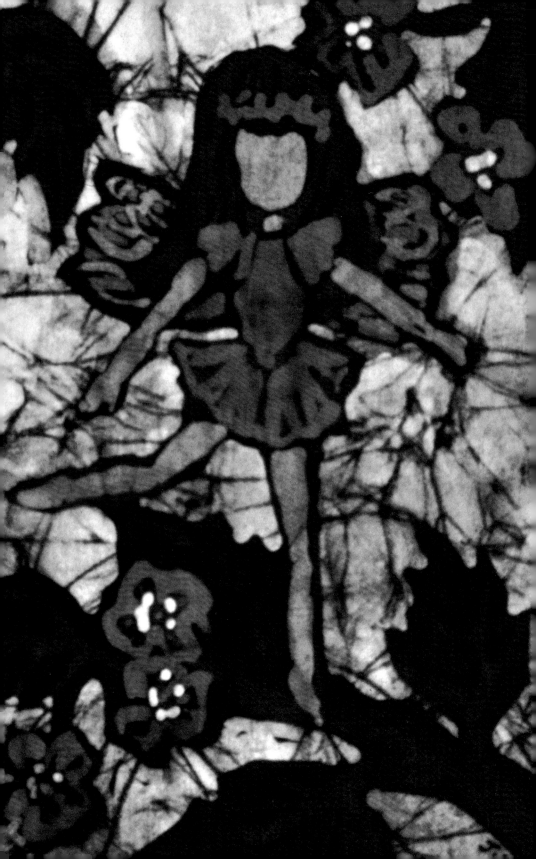

ABOUT THE ART:

Batik is an ancient art that can be traced back 2000 years to India. Batik is a Javanese term meaning "wax writing." Simply, wax is brushed or dripped on the cloth in areas to resist dye. The cloth is then dipped in dye, and after the cloth dries it is waxed again.

During the dyeing process, fine cracks appear in the waxed areas and produce web-like lines that are called "crackling." This is the distinguishing feature neither found, nor possible, in any other textile printing. It is the "crackling" that gives interest and life to Batik paintings.

ABOUT THE ARTIST:

 Jennifer has been creating Batik paintings since 1987. She has exhibited in shows, galleries and museums, and her work is in homes all over the world.

In 2005 she received the award of "Best of Show" in fiber art at the Ann Arbor Art Fair. This story about Clarissa and Betty has been in Jennifer's heart and soul since Jennifer was a child when her mother first told her the story. She will be sharing more stories about Clarissa in the future.

Jennifer and her husband, Don, live in North-west Michigan in the Sleeping Bear Dunes area. They have five children and one granddaughter.

Clarissa's Friend Betty

Betty Jane Povolo
September 7th, 1930 - January 25th, 2007

This book is dedicated to my mother who taught all of her children and grandchildren and great-granddaughter to believe in fairies and all things magical. She also taught us to believe in the creative power that is in each of us.

"All that I am or hope to be I owe to my mother" - Abraham Lincoln